ANTELOPE

Jenny

by

FRANCES MARY HENDRY

Illustrated by Maureen Bradley

HAMISH HAMILTON
LONDON

HAMISH HAMILTON LTD

Published by the Penguin Group
27 Wrights Lane, London w8 5tz, England
Viking Penguin Inc., 375 Hudson Street, New York, New York 10014, USA
Penguin Books Australia Ltd, Ringwood, Victoria, Australia
Penguin Books Canada Ltd, 2801 John Street, Markham, Ontario, Canada l3r 1b4
Penguin Books (NZ) Ltd,182–190 Wairau Road, Auckland 10, New Zealand

Penguin Books Ltd, Registered Offices: Harmondsworth, Middlesex, England

First published in Great Britain by
Hamish Hamilton Ltd 1991

Copyright © 1991 by Frances Mary Hendry
Illustrations copyright © 1991 by Maureen Bradley

A cip catalogue record for this book is available from the British Library

isbn 0-241-13034-4

Typeset by Rowland Phototypesetting Ltd,
Bury St Edmunds, Suffolk
Printed in Great Britain by
BPCC Hazell Books
Aylesbury, Bucks, England
Member of BPCC Ltd.

Jenny and the Strip-tease Baby

JENNY'S BABY SISTER Ellen was a proper little pest.

She didn't cry often. Well, not terribly often. She didn't sick up, or throw her food about, or pull your hair, or draw on the walls.

She didn't keep everybody awake at night banging on her cot.

In the supermarket she didn't grab for things on the low shelves.

The real trouble with her was that she kept taking off her clothes.

The first time was on a train. Ellen was two years old. Mum took her eyes off her for just a second and she vanished.

"Lordy Lord, where's she gone to?" Mum said to Jenny.

Suddenly a woman stood up, laughing, at a table a few seats along.

"Has anybody lost a baby?" she called out.

Mum was already heading that way. "Yes, me!" she said grimly.

Ellen smiled up at them. She had pulled off her dress and vest.

"See!" she said proudly, sticking out her tummy. "See my tummy-button!"

Everybody except Mum roared with laughter. Mum was black affronted.

That summer, Ellen loved going to the paddling pool on the Links. She kept wanting to go, even when nobody had time to take her. So she started to go alone.

The pool wasn't far from the house, just across the grassy Links. She was a clever wee girl, always went straight there, and never got lost. She learned how to open the gate, and when Dad tied it up, she just climbed over the wall and slid down. She was very bad at it.

Or maybe, Jenny thought, she was very good at it?

But Ellen took off her clothes on the way.

Away she ran, happily stripping off her shoes and clothes as she went, till by the time she reached the pool she had nothing on at all.

Mum was at her wits' end, but Ellen was fine. She was never frightened by nasty people or dogs, because everybody in the Fishertown knew her and kept an eye on her. She never even caught a cold.

There was a constant stream of boys and girls at the door.

"Mrs Matheson, Mum sent me to say Ellen's at the pool again!"

Or "Mrs Matheson, is this Ellen's dress?" or vest, or socks, or pants, or shoes.

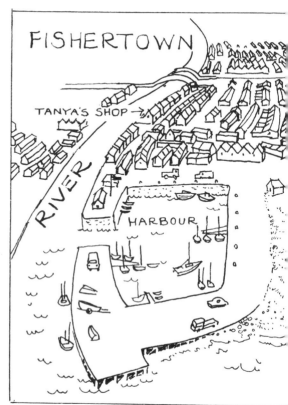

The first snow fell at the end of
January. It was four inches deep, soft
and fluffy all over the streets and
gardens. Jenny and Ellen had a great
time making a snowman, and sledging
with Dad down Bunker's Brae on the
edge of the Links.

Ellen screamed with glee and fright

as she swooped down Bunker's Brae on
Dad's knee. She loved it.

They got home just as it was getting
dark, wet through and tired out.

"Right, you two," said Mum, 'into
the bath! You can have your tea in
your jim-jams and dressing-gowns.
Hurry up!"

Jenny cheered and ran to get her
pyjamas. Dad changed into dry
clothes, and then saw to the sausages
and chips while Mum stripped Ellen

and bathed her and Jenny
double-quick. She rubbed and
powdered Ellen dry, pulled her red
stretchy pyjamas over her head and
went back to the kitchen to help Dad.

"Jenny," Ellen giggled, "go out
again? On sledge?"

She was jumping about like a wee
red devil.

Jenny was wrapping herself in the
big purple towel, and pretending to be
a Roman Emperor in a toga.

"What?" she said. "Out? No, don't
be silly. Go on into the kitchen for tea,
Ellen."

She shoved Ellen gently out of the
bathroom. Only a minute later she
came into the kitchen, all dry and
warm.

"I was just going to call you," said
Mum. "Tea's ready. Where's Ellen?"

There was a nasty pause.

Then Mum fairly leapt out of the door. Up the stairs she ran, into the bedrooms, calling, "Ellen! Ellen!"

No Ellen.

Down again to where Jenny and Dad were looking round the sitting room.

No Ellen.

Mum and Dad looked at each other, and opened the front door. The cold swept in to make Jenny shiver. On the doorstep lay the top half of a pair of red stretchy pyjamas. Down by the open gate lay the trousers.

"Oh, no!" Mum was as white as a sheet.

"Don't worry now, Maggie, I'll find her! Jenny, look after your mum!"

Dad grabbed his coat and dashed off out, calling, "Ellen! Ellen!"

Mum started to go out after him, but Jenny grabbed at her arm.

"Stop, Mum! Put on your coat! It's cold!"

Her mother looked blindly down at her for a second. Then she nodded quickly, and struggled into her sheepskin coat.

"Stay here, now, in case she comes

back! Don't you go out as well!"

She was running down the street before she'd finished.

Jenny closed over the door. She was worried and excited. How daft Ellen was, running off into the snow with no clothes on! She went and put off the gas under the chip pan.

Suddenly she remembered what Ellen had said about the sledge, and her laughing face. She opened the door and checked: yes, the sledge was gone from the corner of the garden!

She shouted for her mum and dad, but nobody answered.

What should she do?

Mum had said to stay here.

But Ellen would be away to Bunker's Brae again, getting colder and colder, and Dad and Mum didn't know where to look for her.

Could Jenny get Danny, or Auntie Kate next door, or anybody? No, there wasn't time.

It was far too cold for Ellen to be out, especially with no clothes on.

No, Jenny had to go herself, right away, whatever Mum had said.

Jenny dragged on her coat over her pyjamas. It was all damp and sticky, but that didn't matter. She tugged on her welly boots. She pulled on a bobble hat over her damp hair, and picked up Ellen's coat and wellies. She'd need them if she found her.

Then she stepped out into the snow and closed the door, and ran as fast as she could for Bunker's Brae.

Jenny slipped and slithered on the ice. Her hands and feet were freezing, though the rest of her was quite hot with running.

She was calling all the time, "Ellen! Where are you? Ellen!"

But there was no answer.

As she reached the corner of the Links she saw something dark on the snow beyond the pillar-box ahead.

It was the sledge. She was on the right track!

She took the sledge with her, and ran even faster along the road beside

the Links. There was a little figure, all
alone, standing in the snow under a
lamp.

It was Ellen.

Jenny nearly started to cry with
relief.

Ellen was shivering hard, whimpering, blue with cold. She was so cold she couldn't speak.

Jenny wrapped Ellen's coat round her, and put her wee boots on her, and sat her down on the sledge to take her home. She took off her bobble hat and put it on Ellen, warm from her own head.

It wasn't enough. Ellen was still shivering.

Jenny started to take off her own coat as well. The cold made her shudder, but Ellen needed it more than she did. She'd just have to manage without it.

Suddenly there was a shout quite close.

"Ellen! Ellen! Are you there?"

It was Dad.

"Dad!" yelled Jenny. "We're here! Over here!"

She was so happy to hear his voice!

Dad came panting up out of the darkness, and didn't stop to ask any silly questions. He just picked them both up, tucked them inside his warm coat, and rushed them straight home.

Mum was there, standing at the open door with Danny and Auntie Kate. When she saw them she started to laugh and cry together. It was a horrible noise, but after a minute it changed to just crying.

Jenny was a bit surprised, and hurt. She thought Mum would have been glad to see them. Then she remembered how she had felt when she saw Ellen, and she knew Mum was crying out of happiness and relief.

They were dumped in another hot bath, and the doctor came. He checked them carefully, and said they were both well. No frostbite, not even a sniffle. It was a miracle.

Then they were tucked up in bed and Mum had another good cry.

Jenny was very pleased about three things.

First, Dad went out and bought her fish and chips from the shop, because the tea he had made was all spoiled, and she had it on a tray in bed like a lady.

Next, Mum let her have a special treat; a big plate of ice-cream with pears and chocolate sauce and scooshy cream, for having saved Ellen.

But the best thing of all was that Ellen never did a strip-tease again.

Jenny and the Mouse that Liked Soap

ONE DAY, JENNY'S Mum opened the pantry door and said, "Lordy Lord! Would you just look at that!"

Jenny looked. "What is it, Mum?" she asked. She couldn't see anything dreadful.

"Those wee black things on the shelf!" said Mum. "They're mouse droppings! We've got mice!"

Jenny rather liked the idea of a mouse in the house. But Mum didn't.

"I wonder what else they've been chewing at," she said, and hunted all through the cupboards.

The mice had eaten holes in a box of cornflakes, and a packet of biscuits, and a woolly cardigan Mum had knitted for Baby Ellen. That really made her angry.

"Where are they getting in?" she wondered.

Suddenly there was a quick scurry across the floor.

"There it is, Mum!" shouted Jenny.

A tiny, little grey mouse with huge, big ears and a long, thin tail scuttled into the cupboard under the sink.

Mum picked up a brush and opened the cupboard carefully, ready to hit the mouse if it ran out again. But it didn't.

She gently took out the bucket and brushes and the bag of soap that she left there to dry out. There was a little hole right in the far corner.

"Right!" Mum said. "There'll be a

trap down for you tomorrow." Then she looked more carefully at the soap bag. "Here, Jenny, look at this!" she said.

There were six bars of different kinds of soap in the bag. The mouse had bitten a hole in the bag, and started to chew the soap. It had taken a nibble or two at all the soaps, but only one bar was badly gnawed. It was half eaten away.

"Boy, it must have been hungry!" said Jenny. "I wonder if the soap foamed up in its tummy!"

"I wonder what the makers would say if we sent it to them," she said. "They could use it in an advert. *99% of mice in our tests preferred this soap!*"

Mum laughed too. "Let's try it!" she said.

She helped Jenny write the letter to

the manufacturers. They carefully
wrapped up the half-eaten bar of soap,
and posted the parcel next day on their
way up to Jenny's school.

That very same day, Mum brought
home a mousetrap.

"Get me a bit of bacon, Jenny," said
Mum. "They say bacon's better than
cheese."

She tried to pull back the bar, but it was so strong she couldn't get it pinned down.

"Hoy, Bill!" she called to Dad. "This is too stiff. Will you set it for me?"

"I thought you Liberated Women could do anything!" Dad joked.

But he took the trap and pulled back the bar. It was strong, but he pinned it down quite easily.

"See? Nothing to it!" he boasted.

He took the bit of bacon, and stuck it down on the pin. He must have pressed too hard, or his fingers were slippy with the bacon fat, or something. The clip opened, and the bar slammed down on his thumb.

"Yee-ow!" he yelled.

"It works well, doesn't it?" said Mum.

Dad danced round the kitchen for quite some time till the pain went down. His thumb was all red.

Jenny had a hard time not to laugh. But she knew it wouldn't be kind. So she didn't.

Mum did.

So did Dad, after a while.

At last they managed to get the trap set properly. They put it carefully in the cupboard beside the soap.

Next morning, Mum went to look at it.

It had been sprung. The bar was down. The bacon was gone. But the mouse hadn't been caught.

Mum and Dad tried again the next few nights. The bait was always gone in the morning, and the trap sprung. But the mouse wasn't caught.

"Lordy Lord!" said Mum. "A right

smart mouse we've got here!"

At last they decided the mousetrap was useless, in spite of the way it had trapped Dad's thumb.

Jenny was quite pleased. She'd been afraid they would hear her creeping down the stairs to set the trap off and put out more food for the mouse so that it wouldn't need to bite holes in things.

Then Dad had an idea. "I've been thinking," he announced one morning.

"Oh dear, was it very sore?" asked Mum.

"Grrr!" Dad shouted, and chased her all over the kitchen till he caught her and gave her a big kiss. "Now let that be a lesson to you," he said firmly, and as Mum started to say something else he went on fast. "We'll borrow a cat."

"Borrow a cat?" Mum was quite surprised.

"Just for a few days. To get rid of the mouse!" Dad explained.

Mum thought about it for a minute. It wasn't a bad idea at all.

That night Mum asked Miss Bochel across the road if they could have a loan of her cat. So Ginger came to stay.

Ginger was a big, thin, tough cat. He had a great reputation as a mouser.

He also bit Baby Ellen. And scratched the furniture. And Dad. And climbed up the curtains, and tore them. And stole a kipper from the fridge. And sicked it up right in the middle of the carpet.

"Lordy Lord!" said Mum. "That cat's ten times the trouble of the mouse!"

He didn't even catch anything – at least, not that anybody saw.

After three days, Mum took him back to Miss Bochel and politely said, "Thank you very much."

Jenny was very pleased. She'd rather have the mouse any day. She'd been quite worried about it while the cat was there.

Dad's next idea was rat poison.

"What? In a house with a child and a baby in it? Over my dead body!" Mum said.

"Drat! That's why I wanted it!" Dad whispered loudly to Jenny. Mum pretended to hit him with the frying pan she was washing, and spilled soapy water all over the floor.

Dad and Jenny had a good laugh.

"Well," said Dad, "I can block up the hole, at least."

He went up to the D-I-Y shop in the High Street, and bought a can of plastic foam that set hard.

"We'll jam twisted wire into the hole, and then scoosh in the foam. If the mice try to chew it, they'll not get through the wire," he said.

Dad let Jenny do the filling. It was just like putting cream on a trifle. Jenny didn't mind it at all, because she wasn't hurting the mouse.

That night, Jenny came down quietly to the kitchen and sat down beside the sink cupboard.

"Mouse!" she whispered. "Mouse! Can you hear me? I like you, but Mum doesn't. If you stay here she and Dad'll get you somehow. Please, mouse, go away."

The mouse didn't answer, of course.

A few days later Mum was checking

the cupboards again.

"I do believe we've done it!" she said happily. "Look! Not a sign of mouse droppings in a week. It's gone!"

So it had. And it didn't come back —
at least, not that anybody saw.

Jenny thought that the story of the
mouse was all over.

Then one day a parcel came to the
house, addressed to her. It was square,
and quite heavy.

"What can it be?" she wondered.

"Why not try opening it and find
out?" Dad suggested.

There was a white box in the parcel,
and a letter.

Dear Jenny,

*Thank you for your letter. We have never
had a recommendation quite like this before.
We don't think we can use it in an
advertisement, but we liked reading it very
much. We are sending you some of our most
expensive soap, and hope that your mouse will
enjoy this as much as the last.*

There were a dozen bars of lovely

creamy scented soap in the box.

"The mouse wasn't all bad, Mum, was it?" asked Jenny.

Jenny and the Sari

ONE YEAR NAIRN Drama Club put on a show of costumes from round the world. Mysie, the wardrobe mistress, asked Jenny's mum if she would help.

"Sure, Mysie," said Jenny's mum. "We'll all help. Bill can stir himself to do the music, won't you, Billy boy?" She knocked on the top of his head. "Hello? Anybody in down there?"

Jenny's dad rubbed his head and growled. "I suppose I'll have to! Just let me know what you want, and I'll make up a tape for you."

Jenny was playing Ludo with her

friend, Mary, from next door.

"Can I be in it, Mum?" asked Jenny.

"Me too," said Mary.

"Oh, I think we can find something to fit you," said Mysie with a smile.

They all went down to the Drama Club store to look through the costumes.

"There's the Egyptian belly-dancer, and the Spanish mantillas," said Mysie. "And there's that Siamese costume with the glittery gold head-dress. One of the girls could wear that, it's small."

"Bags I!" shouted Mary right away.

Jenny was a bit huffed.

"And Jenny could wear the smallest kimono from *The Mikado*, the red one with the black dragons, and a black wig with flowers at the side."

Jenny made a face at Mary. Dragons and a flowery wig were just as good as gold hats.

"Right," said Dad. "That's Egyptian music, full of Eastern Promise!" He rolled his eyes and wobbled his hips to make them laugh. "And something Spanish, no problem. But Japanese or Siamese music? Where do I get that, eh?"

"*The King and I!*" shouted Jenny. "*The March of the Siamese Children!*"

Dad smacked her bottom gently, just in fun. "Great! Perfecto! But you needn't shout, Jenny. We're not in Inverness!"

Slowly lots of costumes were hunted out, tried on, ironed and hung up.

Mum chased Dad till he made up music for an interesting show.

But there weren't enough countries.

"Look," said Mum one night. "My sister's sent me some silk from India. It's a real sari. Does anybody know how to put it on?"

But nobody did, not even Mysie. They tried it all ways, but it just looked silly and lumpy, not graceful as it should do.

Next day Jenny was swinging on the gate, because her dad wasn't there to tell her not to, when a little girl came up the street. She had the loveliest dress Jenny had ever seen. It looked like a single piece of cloth wrapped round her, bright red, with gold along the bottom edge.

Jenny stared.

The girl stopped and stared back. The pleats at the front of her dress were coming loose. She wound the cloth up round her hand, without needing to look, and stuffed it back into her waistband.

"Hello," Jenny said. "What's your name?"

"Hassina," said the little girl. "That's one of them. I've got two names. Hassina is one, and Sekri is the other. Hassina Sekri. Have you got two names too?"

"Yes, of course I have," said Jenny. "Everybody has. Mine are Jennifer Agnes Matheson."

"That's three names," said the little girl. She grinned.

"So it is," Jenny grinned back. "I love your dress," she said. "I wish I had one like it."

The little girl looked pleased. "It's a sari," she said.

"A sari!" Jenny said. "That's magic! Hassina, can you come and show my mum how to put it on?"

The little girl grinned again, and came in shyly. She tried to show Mum how to arrange the long cloth. She could manage her own little cotton sari fine, but she was too small to handle Mum's wide, slippery silk.

At last Mum shook her head. "No, this won't work. Hassina, do you think your own mother would show me?"

"Oh, yes, she'll be happy to!" said Hassina. "Come on home with me."

Jenny didn't know what to expect. She was a bit disappointed to find that Hassina's house was just like her own, but a bit bigger and brighter. There were lots of pictures, and Christmas decorations even in summer. A video of an Indian lady dancing was on the television in one corner.

There were toys everywhere and

four little boys. Hassina explained that her mum's sister and her family lived there too.

Mrs Sekri gave them a cup of tea and some sweet, sticky cakes. Jenny had never tasted anything like them

before. They were lovely, even nicer than chocolate digestives.

Hassina's Mum didn't speak much English, and her aunt spoke none at all, so Hassina had to translate for them.

Mrs Sekri put the sari on Jenny's mum properly.

"Is this right?" asked Mum, trying it for herself.

It all fell off, and everybody laughed.

"Oh, I'm no good at it, but you make it look so easy!" She tried again and again.

Mrs Sekri nodded and smiled as Mum got it right at last.

"Mrs Sekri," said Jenny's mum, "would you like to be in the show yourself? You could wear your own sari and jewellery, and show people what it should really look like. Maybe

you could even do an Indian dance,
like the one on the video. You'd be
beautiful."

Jenny thought this was a very good
idea, and so did Hassina, but Mrs
Sekri smiled, and shook her head. She
said she would like to, but she was
going to have a baby soon, and could
not dance.

"Well, can Hassina come, then?"
asked Jenny.

Hassina jumped up and down at the
idea.

They had to wait till next day, till
Mr Sekri could be asked, but at last it
was all agreed. Hassina was very
happy.

On the night of the show Jenny and
her mum and Mary went to Hassina's
house to take her to the theatre very
early to get into their first costumes.

Dad came along too, to see how his tape sounded.

The first costumes on show were Spanish, long and frilly, and the girls wearing them did a slinky dance with castanets.

Then Jenny and Mary took part in a dance from Russia, with waving handkerchiefs and lots of stamping. It was very fast and noisy.

After it came a slow, creepy scene, with an ancient statue from Peru coming alive.

Next there was another fast, bright scene when one of the girls did a gipsy dance with a tambourine, while the rest changed into their Eastern clothes.

Mary's pointed gold hat was very heavy and uncomfortable, and had to be padded out with foam to keep it on her head. She had gold trousers and a red top with gold braid.

Jenny had her red dragon kimono and a Japanese fan to wave.

Mysie had found Hassina a small blue kimono and a parasol so that she could be in this scene too.

Mary had to walk on first, with high, slow steps, keeping her toes pointing up, and hoping her hat didn't fall off. Then the ladies in kimonos glided on, with Hassina and Jenny, and they all did a dance together with lots of bowing.

Mary didn't bow, of course, or her hat would have come off.

There were lots of scenes. In one, everybody dressed as Maoris and did a hula-hula. There was a scene in America with the best dancer doing the Charleston. There was the belly-dance.

In the English one King Henry the Eighth danced a slow, stately dance to the tune of *Greensleeves* with a lady wearing a huge satin dress and a ruff round her neck. It was very elegant.

The dressing-room behind the stage was very different. Everybody was rushing about like crazy, getting changed in a mad panic, zipping each other up and down and shouting in whispers, "Where's my shoes?" – or necklace or fan or hat!

The last scene was the one where the saris were to be shown. Mary and Jenny, in two of Hassina's small saris, came in and stood one on each side of the stage.

Jenny's mum wore her own sari. She and Hassina did a dance to Indian music.

Then Jenny's mum pulled off the

sari cloth, so that she was just in her blouse and petticoat, and showed how to put it on, just as Mrs Sekri had shown her.

The audience were very interested.

Right at the end, everybody came on in their favourite costume, Spanish frills or Maori grass skirt, Japanese kimono or Indian sari, to wave goodbye to the audience, who clapped and cheered, especially when Hassina and Mary and Jenny made their bows.

All the audience said as they were going home that it was the young ones who had been the stars of the show. They had looked so happy, as if they were really enjoying themselves.

Jenny wondered why there was such a fuss.

Of course they'd been enjoying themselves!

Jenny and the Weather Witch

TANYA KEPT AN antique shop in
Harbour Street. There were beautiful
plates and ornaments, and glass and
jewellery, and a peacock with a long
shimmering tail.

Mum said Tanya was artistic. She
wore brighter clothes and more
make-up than anybody else. She liked
big, wide, feathery hats, and laughed
loudly, a lot.

Jenny loved to watch her. She
spread a kind of warm glow all round
her.

But Jenny was surprised to find out

that Tanya was a weather witch.

The weather had been horrible for three whole weeks.

Jenny was coming home from school with her mum and wee Ellen, jumping over the puddles.

Just as they passed Tanya's shop, Tanya came out, bright as one of her stuffed birds.

Suddenly the sun started to shine.

"Hello, Tanya!" said Jenny's mum. "I like your hat!"

The blue feathers on it flashed in the new sunshine as Tanya kissed her – she always kissed everybody.

"Lordy Lord, you're brown! Did you have a good time in Morocco?" said Mum. "You've brought the sun back with you, anyway."

Tanya bent down to kiss Jenny too, and Jenny laughed. Tanya's lipstick

was scarlet and her gold earrings jingled like bells. It was a bit silly, being kissed by somebody who wasn't your family, but scented and rather nice.

The sunlight seemed even brighter.

"Why, have you had a lot of rain, dear?" Tanya asked.

"Ever since you left, as usual. It always rains when you're away."

They both laughed, and Jenny's mum pushed the pram on down Harbour Street.

"Did Tanya really bring the sun back, Mum?" Jenny asked.

"What? Lordy Lord, no, lassie!" said Mum. "I was just making a wee joke that she took the good weather with her."

But Jenny remembered – when Tanya was away at Easter, a dreadful storm had blown down a chimney. So maybe it was true, but her mum didn't want to tell her. Grown-ups were like that, sometimes. It was a nice thought, that while Tanya was in town the weather would most likely be good. She was glad Tanya was back.

Next Saturday the rain was fairly lashing down. Jenny wondered where Tanya was.

Jenny's friend Danny had a boat that he used to catch lobsters. He had a stove in the cabin and he often made Jenny a cup of tea. Jenny decided this was a good day to go down to the harbour to see him.

Her new yellow plastic oilskins had a funny new smell. Mum told her to be careful, because her old blue wellies leaked, but she scooshed through some very deep puddles just for fun. The

trickles down between her toes felt
tickly.

Tanya was loading big cardboard
boxes into her estate car.

"Are you going away again, Tanya?" Jenny asked, helping to push in a box. Of course, this was why it was raining so hard, she thought.

"Yes, down to a sale in Edinburgh. Thanks, dear. Drat this rain! The boxes are going all squodgy. And would you look at my poor hat!" Tanya tossed her head so that spray flew off the drooping red feathers, and laughed.

Danny wasn't at the harbour. He was out in his boat at his lobster pots. Jenny hung about waiting for him.

Some men with a big crane were lifting boats out of the water onto a lorry, to be stored away for the winter. Jenny watched them for a while.

The rain dribbled and dripped off the edge of her yellow oilskins until she was standing in a circle of puddle.

There was a leak on her right shoulder, and if she bent her head the sou'wester hat poured the rain down her neck. A wind started to flurry her oilskins and her denims got damp and stuck to her legs. She was chilly and damp, and drips were dripping off her nose. She decided this was no fun; she'd not wait any longer.

Then Mr Main the harbourmaster came out and hoisted a big black cone on the mast beside his office.

Jenny went over to find out what it was.

"It's blown up all of a sudden out of nowhere," Mr Main was saying to the men. "The weather men say it'll be gusting to gale force ten or eleven."

"That's a right nasty wind," one of the men replied. "Any boats out?"

"Just Danny. He'll not be long now,

when he sees the storm cone up."

Jenny was worried. Danny could be in trouble. His boat was old, and it might sink in a storm. What would Danny do then, with no boat? Or maybe he might even get drowned!

Suddenly she thought of Tanya. If Tanya would stay, maybe the weather wouldn't be so bad, and Danny would get home safe.

Could she keep her back somehow?

Tanya was just opening the car door to drive away. What could Jenny do to hold her back?

A strong gust of wind whistled up the street. The feathers of Tanya's hat flapped wildly. It blew off her head and sailed away up the road like a huge red frisbee.

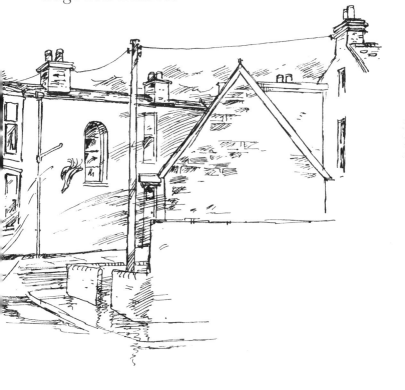

"Oh, drat it!" said Tanya, and took a step after it.

Jenny's yellow oilskins clattered as she raced past Tanya.

"I'll get it for you!" she called. "You can come after me in your car!"

Tanya laughed, and shouted, "All right! I'm right behind you!"

What a chase that was!

The red hat seemed to have a life of its own. Every time Tanya thought Jenny must sure have caught it, it flew off in a different direction. Up along Harbour Street, and then down to the side of the river. Tanya thought surely it would go into the water, but no, there was Jenny waving from further along beside the amusement arcade. Then back down Harbour Street, and round the twisty wee lanes behind the Brackla Hotel.

Tanya kept finding the car couldn't get through the narrow passages and she had to go back and find a new way through. Every time she was ready to give up, there was Jenny waving, and the red hat flying along in a new direction, and she would swing the wheel round and wriggle the car after them again.

The wind must be gusting very, very hard round all the corners, she thought. It was almost as if somebody was throwing the hat about!

At long last the hat flew down near the harbour, landed and rolled, and a man standing by the quayside trapped it under his foot.

Jenny came round the corner after it and stopped running with a gasp. It was Mr Main. That was that.

Well, she'd done her best to keep

Tanya there. Had it been long enough? She looked down into the harbour basin, and sighed with relief. Danny's boat was just easing gently up to the quay wall.

Danny tossed up a rope to the harbourmaster.

"Aye, aye, Danny! You just made it," called Mr Main, tying the rope round one of the big iron mooring rings at his feet.

"Getting a bit rough, eh?" Danny replied.

He heaved up a big plastic bucket of crabs to Mr Main just as Tanya's car drew up beside them and Tanya climbed out.

"Rough? Well, there's a fair gale due. It should have been here by now!" Mr Main said.

Then he turned to Tanya and handed her the hat.

"This would be your hat, then, eh, Tanya? Lucky it didn't go in the water."

It dripped miserably between Tanya's finger and thumb. The red feathers were broken and filthy.

"Thank you," she said with a
sideways twist to her mouth. "It's just
what I always wanted."

"It's a bit bashed, though, eh?"
Danny was grinning up at them all.
"Was Jenny catching it for you?"

"I'm sorry, Tanya," Jenny muttered. Her face was all red. She hoped Tanya would think it was from the running. "Will it not clean up?"

Suddenly Tanya laughed. "No, dear, it won't. But I never liked it much, anyway. The wind can have it!"

In the blasts that were growing stronger all the time her hair was swirling out in black coils round her head. Her long gold earrings swung and gleamed.

She really looked just like a witch, Jenny thought.

Tanya drew back her arm and, laughing, tossed the poor hat up, up, to where the wind could catch it and swirl it further up and away, right up over the pier and then away out of sight.

Then she glanced at her watch.

"Heavens, dear, just look at the
time!" she cried. "I'll never make
Edinburgh by two o'clock if I don't go.
Now don't you worry, Jenny; you did
your best. 'Bye!"

She kissed Jenny as usual, jumped into the car and drove off very fast.

Danny tied up his boat carefully, because of the storm coming, and then he and Mr Main walked off up the road with the crabs.

Jenny followed them. She was sorry about Tanya's fancy hat. But it had been in a good cause, and it had worked. She had done her best, just as Tanya had said.

Just as Jenny turned in to her own gate, there was a howl of wind. It nearly pushed her off her feet.

"Come in quick and shut the door over, lassie!" said Mum. "Would you like to make us all some tea? It looks like you're home just in time. There's a right strong gale blowing up."

"Yes, Mum," said Jenny. "I saw Mr Main put up the storm cone. But

Danny's boat got in all right."

She smiled to herself as she took off her wellies and went to put on the kettle.

Tanya hadn't gone when she meant to, and the storm had stayed away long enough for Danny to get in safe.

Now she knew for sure that Tanya was a weather witch.

Jenny and the Pantomime Camel

JENNY AND MARY went to the pantomime in the Little Theatre every year. Their mums helped to put it on.

Last year Jenny's mum said to her, "Kate and I thought that we'd take you and Mary along to the rehearsals with us, if you promise to keep very quiet and be very good. Would you like that?"

What a silly question!

Jenny was surprised at all the work that had to be done.

It wasn't just that the cast had to

learn their words and their moves. All the costumes had to be made and fitted, ironed and kept tidy, and all the jewellery and sashes and shoes to go with them. All the scenery had to be made, and painted fresh and bright, and the props – that was the crowns and rocks and thrones and so on – gathered together.

Jenny and Mary helped John, the stage manager, make the props. Or the producer, Anne, sometimes let them sit next to her and watch the rehearsal. They saw it so often, they even started to learn the songs and dances.

Jenny asked, "Can we have a part, please, Anne?"

"Not this year, you're too small. When you're in the big school, if you're still keen," Anne said.

"That's not fair!" whispered Mary.

Auntie Kate played the hero, who was called the Principal Boy, in a lovely gold and silver coat.

A big fat man called Sandy played
the Dame, Nanny MacAroon. He had
a red and yellow tartan dress with a
huge pad called a bustle round his
bottom.

When the Dame, who was a man, was fluttering her – or was it his? – eyelashes at the Principal Boy, who was a lady, it was very confusing.

One of the scenes had a camel in it.

A Pantomime Camel, of course, not a real one. It was acted by two girls from the big school. They rehearsed with a sheet over their heads until their costume was ready.

The camel had a queer kind of walk – both feet on the same side together – and it could nod and shake its head and wink at the audience. It knelt down with just its front legs, and sat down with the back ones, and curtseyed with all four together.

The camel had to do a dance with Nanny MacAroon, who hit it with her umbrella. Jenny and Mary laughed till they nearly fell off the seats.

"Come on, Mary, let's try it!" said Jenny.

They got up in the space between the seats and started to do the dance.

Mary did the front legs and head, and Jenny did the back legs and the hump. They danced up and down till Anne told them to stop their carry-on.

Only a month before the show was due to start, Anne was getting very worried.

"Drat those girls! They're not here again!" she said. "Mary and Jenny, will you try acting the camel, so that the rest of us can rehearse the scene?"

"We'd love to!" shouted Jenny and Mary.

Anne was very pleased with them, and they did the camel often after that when the big girls weren't there.

"Well, acting the camel's a change from acting the goat!" said Auntie Kate.

The camel's name was Bella. It meant 'beautiful'.

Its head was made of wire and polystyrene and old stockings, with a droopy nose, tennis balls for eyes and long black eyelashes. It had Christmas tree bells for earrings. There was a huge pink bow stitched on top of the 'hump' bit, and when you pulled its tail, a long rope of Christmas tinsel came out.

The camel costume was made of two old yellow sheets. One sheet had stripes and the other had flowers. It had huge football socks on its feet. It looked very funny indeed.

Just a week before the show Mysie, the wardrobe mistress, was pinning purple and green glittery bows on Jenny's mum's orange dress. Anne came in in a flaming temper.

"Those girls!" she said. "They've dropped out of the show!"

"What? Ouch!" Jenny's mum had jumped so much that Mysie stuck a pin in her.

"Nobody can learn the part in time," said Anne. "We'll have to cut out the camel altogether!"

Auntie Kate and Jenny's mum looked at each other. Then they looked over at Jenny and Mary who were helping John staple cushions onto a throne. Then they looked back at Anne again.

"Er – Anne . . . " said Auntie Kate. "There might be a way . . . "

Mary and Jenny got a big surprise that evening. Anne asked them to do the camel scene again. Everybody was there, watching.

At the end, Anne looked round at the others. "Well?" she asked.

The whole cast started to clap and cheer.

"Great!" shouted John with a huge grin. "It'll be the smallest camel ever!"

"What d'you mean?" the girls said.

"Would you like to do the camel in the show?" asked Anne.

"In the pantomime? For real? Oh, yes, please!" they shouted.

"Come along into the dressing-room, girls, and try on the costume," said Mysie.

The head was quite heavy, but

Mary could just manage to nod and shake it, and pull the cords to make it wink.

The sheets drooped on the floor all round them.

Mysie laughed, and said, "It could be worse. I suppose! Stand still till I pin you up."

She rolled up the legs of the costume about ten times and folded in a foot on each side. Jenny was a bit worried, but she didn't get any pins stuck in her.

On the first night, Jenny and Mary were scared stiff. They put on their costume and sat very quietly in the dressing-room. The others were rushing about putting on their costumes and make-up and talking too much and too loud and too fast.

"How do you feel, lass?" Jenny's mum asked her.

"Very funny. My throat's all dry and my middle's all empty," said Jenny.

"Don't worry, love," said Auntie Kate, pinning her own hair up under her white prince's wig. "We all feel like that."

"You too?" asked Jenny. It wasn't quite so bad if she wasn't the only one.

"Every time. It's stage fright," said Anne. "It's a good thing, really, because it sort of peps you up. If you didn't feel it, you wouldn't act so well."

"Do you feel it too? But you're not on in the show!" said Mary.

"That's the worst of all!" said Anne. "Everything that you do tonight is because of what I've taught you to do. If you make a mess of it, it's my fault. And there's nothing I can do about it now!"

Anne was very nervous at first, but after a while she felt happier.

"It's going well," she whispered to Mary and Jenny. "The audience are laughing! They're enjoying themselves."

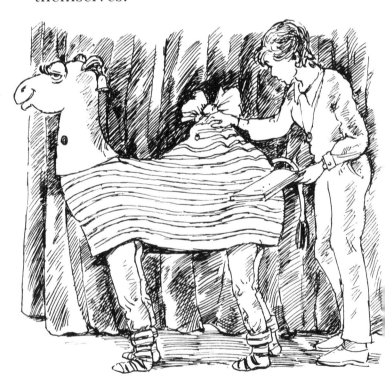

"I wish we were," Jenny whispered to Mary.

They could hear all the jokes that they knew so well coming through the curtains from the stage, but now they didn't want to laugh. They looked at each other and bit their lips, and their hands were shaking.

"I'm scared! I don't want to go on!" whispered Mary.

"We've got to!" Jenny whispered back.

Anne gave them a pat on the hump.

"On you go, now," she said. "You'll be fine!" She crossed her fingers. She hoped she was right!

Jenny was nearly too scared to go onto the stage. She sat down with a bump, because her knees had gone all wobbly. Mary sat on her feet, and the man playing Bella's owner, Ali Qa'at, leaned back on top of them both, as if he was sleeping on the camel as a pillow.

The audience all laughed like crazy. Jenny suddenly felt happy and warm, and wasn't afraid any more.

They remembered all the moves, and didn't trip over the folds of the costume, and didn't fall off the stage. The camel's dance was so funny the audience demanded an encore.

Jenny kept sticking her head, which was the hump, out to the side so that she could see round the camel's head. It looked very funny from the front. Behind the side curtains Anne was grinning all over her face.

At the end of the scene, Ali Qa'at turned to Bella.

"Come, my transport of delight," he said to the camel. "Here is a passenger for you!"

It was the Dame!

Great big fat Sandy was three times the size of this tiny wee camel. The audience roared with laughter when the camel shook its head hard, and then ran away off the stage, and Ali Qa'at pulled its tail and all the gold tinsel came out.

Last thing of all, after everything ended happily ever after, of course, was the Finale. Everybody came on stage in order, smallest parts first, to get their last applause from the audience.

The camel, being a very small part, was one of the first to come on – but Jenny and Mary got one of the loudest cheers.